How Many Fingers?

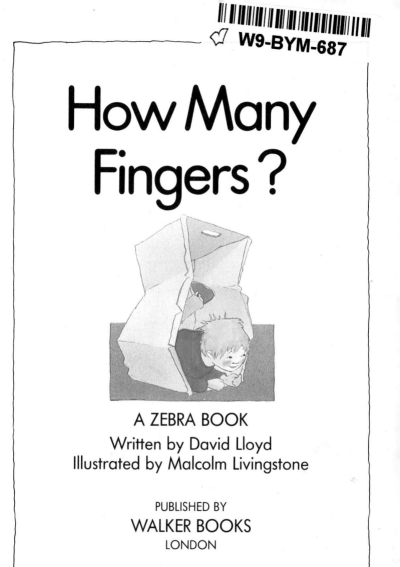

A ZEBRA BOOK

Written by David Lloyd
Illustrated by Malcolm Livingstone

PUBLISHED BY
WALKER BOOKS
LONDON

Polly said, 'I'll be Mrs Humphreys.
She teaches counting.
You do what I say.'
Ben cuddled Big Frog.

Polly took Big Frog.
'This is one,' she said.
'Count one on your fingers.'
Ben looked at Polly
between his legs.

Polly held Big Frog and Rag Doll.
'These are two,' she said.
'Count two on your fingers.'
Ben covered his eyes
with his hands.

'It's time for counting,'
Polly said. 'I'm Mrs Humphreys.
How many fingers is this?'
Ben covered his ears
with his hands.

'How many fingers?' Polly said.
She wrote something important
in the yellow drawing book.
Ben went back to Big Frog.

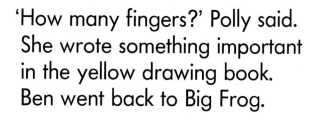

Ben looked up from under
Big Frog and did something difficult
with his fingers.
'Mrs Humphreys says that's about
six fingers,' Polly said.

'Everyone has a desk at school,'
Polly said.
She gave Ben a box for a desk.
She sat Big Frog beside him.
'Good morning, class,' she said.

'This is one and this is one,'
Polly said.
'One and one make two.'
Ben made a noise inside the box.
'BUB! BUB!'
It was a big, soft, frog noise.

'Come out, Ben,' Polly said.
'Mrs Humphreys says come out.'
Polly started going into the box
to pull Ben out.

For a moment there was
no Mrs Humphreys.
There was no Ben.
There was no counting.
Big Frog and Rag Doll
did nothing.

With a sudden noise the box
started stamping about the room.
'One two miss a few ninety
nine a hundred,' the box said
in Polly's voice.
The box fell over a train.

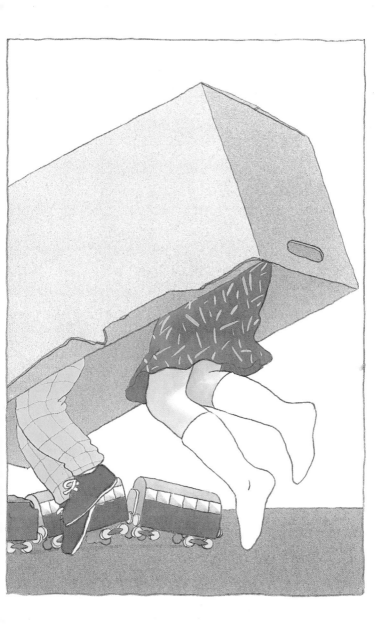

Polly and Ben came out of the box.
'I'm not Mrs Humphreys any
more,' Polly said.

She turned everything into
a hospital.
'You're an ill person with bad
fingers and I'm a doctor,'
she told Ben.

'There there,' Polly said.
'How many fingers are hurting?'
She counted Ben's fingers.
'1 2 3 4 5 6 7 8 9 10.'
Then she bandaged them up.